ANIMAL JUNIOR
CRACKERS

PIPE DOWN, PRUDLE!

ROSE IMPEY ★ SHOO RAYNER

ORCHARD BOOKS

ORCHARD BOOKS
338 Euston Road, London NW1 3BH
Orchard Books Australia
Hachette Children's Books
Level 17/207 Kent Street, Sydney NSW 2000

First published by Orchard Books in 1995
This edition published in 2009

Text © Rose Impey 1995
Illustrations © Shoo Rayner 2002

The rights of Rose Impey to be identified as the author and
Shoo Rayner to be identified as the illustrator of this Work
have been asserted by them in accordance with the
Copyright, Designs and Patents Act, 1988.

A CIP catalogue record for this book is available from the British Library.

ISBN 978 1 40830 511 9

1 3 5 7 9 10 8 6 4 2
Printed in China

Orchard Books is a division of Hachette Children's Books,
an Hachette UK company.
www.hachette.co.uk

Pipe Down, Prudle!

Not all parrots can talk.
Some parrots talk a lot.
Some parrots never know
when to stop.

How do you do?
How do you do?
I'm Prudle the parrot.
Pleased to meet you.

Prudle could talk
the leg off a donkey,

or the tail off a tom cat,

or the ears off an elephant.

Prudle was the most talkative
parrot in the world.

From the moment she woke up
Prudle never closed her beak.
She talked through breakfast

And when it came to bedtime
she was still talking.

Roll over!
Roll over!
Put the kettle on!

Sometimes she even talked
in her sleep.

Lights off!
Lights off!
Put the cat out!

"Pipe down, Prudle,"
everyone shouted.
But Prudle wouldn't.

Prudle belonged to Grandma Bates.
She was her pride and joy.
Grandma Bates taught Prudle to talk.

When she died, she left Prudle,
in her will,
to her grandson, Billy.

But Billy wasn't pleased
to meet Prudle.
Nor was his family.
The Bates family didn't like birds.
They liked television.

They didn't like it
when Prudle talked through
Blue Peter

Sticky-backed
plastic. Here's one
I made earlier.

and *EastEnders*

Load of rubbish!
Leave it out!
Do me a favour!

14

and *Coronation Street.*

By heck, lad. This is bad! Gimme a cup of tea and a barmcake.

She *tried* to talk through *Top of the Pops.*

What a din! Switch it off! Switch it off!

"Someone switch that parrot off,"
said Billy Bates.
"I wish we could," said Mrs Bates.
"Pipe down, Prudle," said the girls.
But Prudle wouldn't.

She talked when Billy Bates
was trying to have a nap...

when his wife was having
coffee with a neighbour…

when Bonnie was playing with her friends…

when Becky had her boyfriend round.

Soon the whole family agreed,
"That parrot will have to go!"

But Prudle liked living
with the Bates family.
No matter how hard they tried
they couldn't get rid of her.

In the end, they found one way
of keeping her quiet.

But one day the Bates family
were glad they couldn't
silence Prudle.
Very glad indeed.

It was a Monday morning.
Mr and Mrs Bates
were late for work.
Bonnie and Becky were late
for school.
The family went out
in such a rush
they left Prudle covered up.

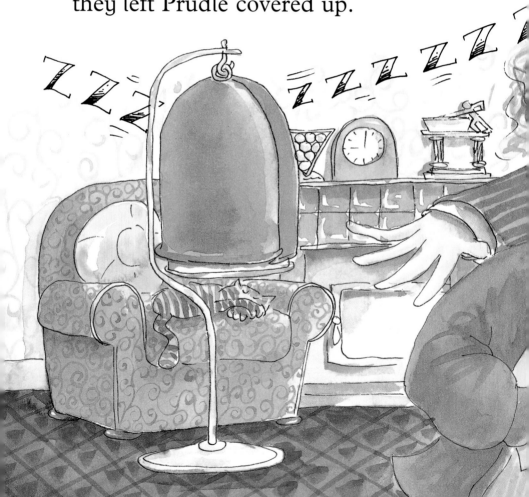

The house was quiet.
The whole street was quiet.
Even Prudle was quiet for a change.
She was still asleep.

Suddenly *someone* put his hand
round the window
and let himself in.

Someone else followed him in.
They were definitely up to no good.

The burglars looked around
to see what they could steal.
They stole Billy Bates's
snooker cups.

They stole Mrs Bates's watch
and the family camera.

They stole Bonnie's computer
and Becky's stereo.

And, as if that wasn't bad enough,
they stole the Bates' television!

They piled them all up
inside the front door.
"Just got time for a drink,"
said the first burglar.
"Coffee or tea?" said the second.
"Hot chocolate," said the first.

The burglars put on the radio
while they had their snack.
The radio woke Prudle up.

The burglars were amazed.
They didn't know where
the noise was coming from.
"Come on, Stan,"
said the first burglar.
"This place gives me the creeps."

"And me, Sid," said the second burglar. "I'm off."

The burglars picked up
the things they had stolen.
They opened the front door
and tried to sneak out.
But Prudle started up again.

The burglars were scared.
"Quick, Stan, you take the telly,"
said Sid.
"Right, Sid. Let's get out of here,"
said Stan, "before the coppers come."

Sid and Stan drove off
in a big red van.
It was full of stolen things.
They had burgled half the houses
in the street.
When everyone came home from work
there was such a fuss.

The police came round.
They took down the details.
They looked for clues
and fingerprints.
"We'll try to find them,"
said the policeman.
But he wasn't very hopeful.

The Bates family was fed up.
Becky had no stereo to listen to.
Bonnie had no computer to play on.
But, worst of all,
they had no television to watch.
The whole family sat there
with nothing to do
and nothing to say.

Except for Prudle of course.
They couldn't keep her quiet.

For a moment there was silence
then Prudle started up again.

This place gives me the creeps.
Gives me the creeps.

The policeman took Prudle's statement.

Sid and Stan were very sorry that
they had burgled the Bates' house.
They were sorry
they had stopped there
for a drink
and a rest.

They had a long time in prison
to feel sorry about it.

After that Prudle was very popular
with the Bates family
and with all their neighbours.
No one tried to keep her quiet now.
In fact, Prudle always had someone
to talk to.

Crack-A-Joke

Why did the robber cut
the legs off his bed?
He wanted to lie low for a while!

What do you use to stuff a parrot?
Polly-filla!

What did the
policeman say
to his tummy?
**You're under
a vest!**

As sick as a parrot!

What happened to
the burglar who stole
a bar of soap?
**He made a
clean getaway!**

What three letters frighten robbers?
I.C.U.

ANIMAL
CRACKERS

COLLECT ALL THE
ANIMAL CRACKERS BOOKS!

All priced at £4.99

Orchard Colour Crunchies are available from all good bookshops, or can be
ordered direct from the publisher:
Orchard Books, PO BOX 29, Douglas IM99 1BQ
Credit card orders please telephone 01624 836000
or fax 01624 837033 or visit our internet site: www.orchardbooks.co.uk
or e-mail: bookshop@enterprise.net for details.
To order please quote title, author and ISBN
and your full name and address.
Cheques and postal orders should be made payable to 'Bookpost plc.'
Postage and packing is FREE within the UK
(overseas customers should add £2.00 per book).
Prices and availability are subject to change.